Wilma
Prua

Little Mouse's Hawaiian Christmas Present

by Mora Ebie illustrated by Holly Braffet

Mutual Publishing

To my daughter, Grace,
the best present I've ever received! —M.E.

For Leif and Gavin —H.B.

ISBN-10: 1-56647-956-8
ISBN-13: 978-1-56647-956-1
Library of Congress Control Number: 2011933372
Design by Jane Gillespie
First Printing, September 2011

Mutual Publishing, LLC
1215 Center Street, Suite 210
Honolulu, Hawai'i 96816
Ph: (808) 732-1709
Fax: (808) 734-4094
e-mail: info@mutualpublishing.com
www.mutualpublishing.com

Printed in China

I t was Christmas Eve, and Little Mouse still hadn't found the perfect present for his mama and papa.

All of his friends had gifts for th
mamas and papas. Little Myn
Bird had woven palm fro
together to make lauha
hats.

Little Seal had gathered
puka shells and made
two beautiful lei.

Little Nēnē Goose had shopped for a handmade one-of-a-kind 'ukulele.

But Little Mouse still couldn't decide what to give his mama and papa.

"Why are you so sad?" asked Little Gecko as Little Mouse passed by with a worried frown.

"It's Christmas Eve and I still haven't found anything for my mama and papa!" cried Little Mouse.

"Oh no!" replied Little Gecko. "I always give my mama and papa the floppiest slippers for Christmas."

Slippers are floppy, thought Little
Mouse, but not perfect for my mama
and papa. He thanked Little Gecko.

As he scampered away, he
bumped into Little Honu.

"Oh, excuse me, Little Honu. I was just looking for a Christmas present for my mama and papa, and I still haven't found anything." Little Mouse muttered.

"Hmmm," said Little Honu. "I decided to buy my mama and papa colorful aloha shirts for Christmas."

Aloha shirts are colorful, thought Little Mouse, but not perfect for my mama and papa.

He thanked Little Honu and started to walk away when he saw his friend, Little Mongoose.

"What's wrong, Little Mouse?" Little Mongoose asked, alarmed at Little Mouse's sad face.

Little Mouse told Little Mongoose about his Christmas present problem. Little Mongoose smiled and said, "I always pick my mama and papa the juiciest pineapples!"

Pineapples are juicy, thought Little Mouse, but not perfect for my mama and papa.

Little Mouse thanked Little
Mongoose and trudged back to his
home in the banyan tree with
a heavy sigh. He still had
not found the perfect
present for his
mama and papa.

"We're glad you're home, Little Mouse," Papa Mouse
said. "We were starting to worry!"
"And it's time for dinner," Mama Mouse announced with
a smile.

But Little Mouse hardly touched any of his cheese
dinner. He was still so sad about not finding the perfect
gift for his mama and papa.

You're not eating your cheese, Little Mouse," Mama Mouse said.
Is something wrong?" asked Papa Mouse.
I'm...just tired," Little Mouse said quietly.
Well, let's all go to bed," Papa Mouse said. "Santa Claus will soon e delivering presents in is sleigh!"

After leaving some cold milk and macadamia nut cookies on a plate by the Christmas tree, Mama and Papa Mouse gave Little Mouse a kiss good-night and tucked him into bed.

But Little Mouse could not sleep a wink. Just then, Little Mouse heard jingling bells and stomping hooves. A bellowing voice boomed, "Ho! Ho! Ho!" It was Santa!

Suddenly, Little Mouse had a wonderful idea! Little Mouse crawled out of bed. He had to talk to Santa before he left.

"Santa, I need your help!" Little Mouse cried. "I looked everywhere for a present for my mama and papa, but I couldn't find the perfect present. Instead of leaving a present for me underneath the tree, can you give me something from your workshop for my mama and papa?"

Santa smiled and patted Little Mouse on top of his head. "Little Mouse, you are a very kind and clever mouse. You don't need a gift from my workshop. You will find the perfect Christmas present for your mama and papa, all by yourself."

And with that, Santa took some bites of warm cookie, a swig of cold milk, and waved goodbye to Little Mouse. Little Mouse suddenly felt very tired, so he climbed into his bed and fell fast asleep.

"Wake up, Little Mouse. It's Christmas morning!" a sweet voice whispered.

Little Mouse's eyes fluttered as he saw Mama and Papa Mouse in his doorway. He looked down at his empty hands. Little Mouse thought about all the adventures his mama and papa had shared with him.

He remembered their trips to find buried treasure, journeys through spooky caves, and even races to the top of the tallest palm tree.

Mama and Papa Mouse were the best mama and papa ever, and Little Mouse had nothing to show his parents how much he loved them. Little Mouse was filled with sadness. He walked to Mama and Papa Mouse and gave them the tightest hug he could.

"Ah, thank you Little Mouse. You gave us the perfect Christmas present!" said Papa Mouse.

Little Mouse looked at his mama and papa with wide eyes. He hadn't given them an 'ukulele, or aloha shirts, or slippers, or puka shells, or pineapples! He had just given them a...hug.

Santa Claus was right! Little Mouse had discovered the perfect present for Mama and Papa Mouse. It hadn't come from the store. It hadn't come from Santa's workshop. It had come from Little Mouse's kind heart.

"Merry Christmas, Mama and Papa," Little Mouse said, and he squeezed them in a tight hug once more.

About the Author

Mora Ebie currently lives in Los Angeles, California, where she spends her time teaching second grade, writing funny stories, planning more visits to the Islands, and spending time with her husband Chris, daughter Grace, and their three mischievous cats, Emma, Schroeder, and Owen.

About the Illustrator

Holly Braffet is a graduate of Moloka'i High and Intermediate School, has a BFA from Ringling College of Art and Design, and an MLIS from UH Mānoa. She is a librarian in Hāna, where she lives with her family and three fat cats. *Little Mouse's Hawaiian Christmas Present* is her fifth book.